The Worst Twelve Days of Christmas

By **Sudipta Bardhan-Quallen**

Illustrated by **Ryan Wood**

Abrams Books for Young Readers
New York

The illustrations in this book were made using pencils and a computer.

Cataloging-in-Publication Data has been applied for and may be obtained from the Library of Congress.
ISBN: 978-1-4197-0033-0

Printed and bound in China
10 9 8 7 6 5 4 3 2 1

Abrams Books for Young Readers are available at special discounts when purchased in quantity for premiums and promotions as well as fundraising or educational use. Special editions can also be created to specification. For details, contact specialmarkets@abramsbooks.com or the address below.

ABRAMS
THE ART OF BOOKS SINCE 1949

115 West 18th Street
New York, NY 10011
www.abramsbooks.com

To Sawyer, my Sam and my joy.
— S. B.

For Logan, Paige, Brooklyn, and Melannie.
— R. W.

It was Joy's sixth Christmas, but it would be Sam's first.
Joy knew this year would surely be the worst.

So . . . with **12** days till Christmas, all that Joy could see
Was a stinky baby messing with the tree.

When Joy found her angel that always tops the tree,
Sam grabbed the wings and then he snapped them free.

So . . . with **11** days till Christmas, all that Joy could see
Were **2** severed wings
and a stinky baby messing with the tree.

After Joy decorated a new wreath for the door,
Sam ripped it up and tossed it on the floor.

So . . . with **10** days till Christmas, all that Joy could see
Were **3** wreath scraps,
2 severed wings
and a stinky baby messing with the tree.

Joy got Sam's first stocking and glitter-glued his name.
He stuck it to the others—what a shame!

So . . . with **9** days till Christmas, all that Joy could see
Were **4** sticky stockings,
3 wreath scraps,
2 severed wings
and a stinky baby messing with the tree.

Joy hung the Christmas mistletoe high above Sam's head.
She puckered up . . . but heard a CRASH instead.

Crash!

So . . . with **8** days till Christmas, all that Joy could see

Were **5** shattered ornaments,

4 sticky stockings,

3 wreath scraps,

2 severed wings

and a stinky baby messing with the tree.

Joy signed all her Christmas cards and left them on the stairs.
Sam grabbed the stack and then began to tear.

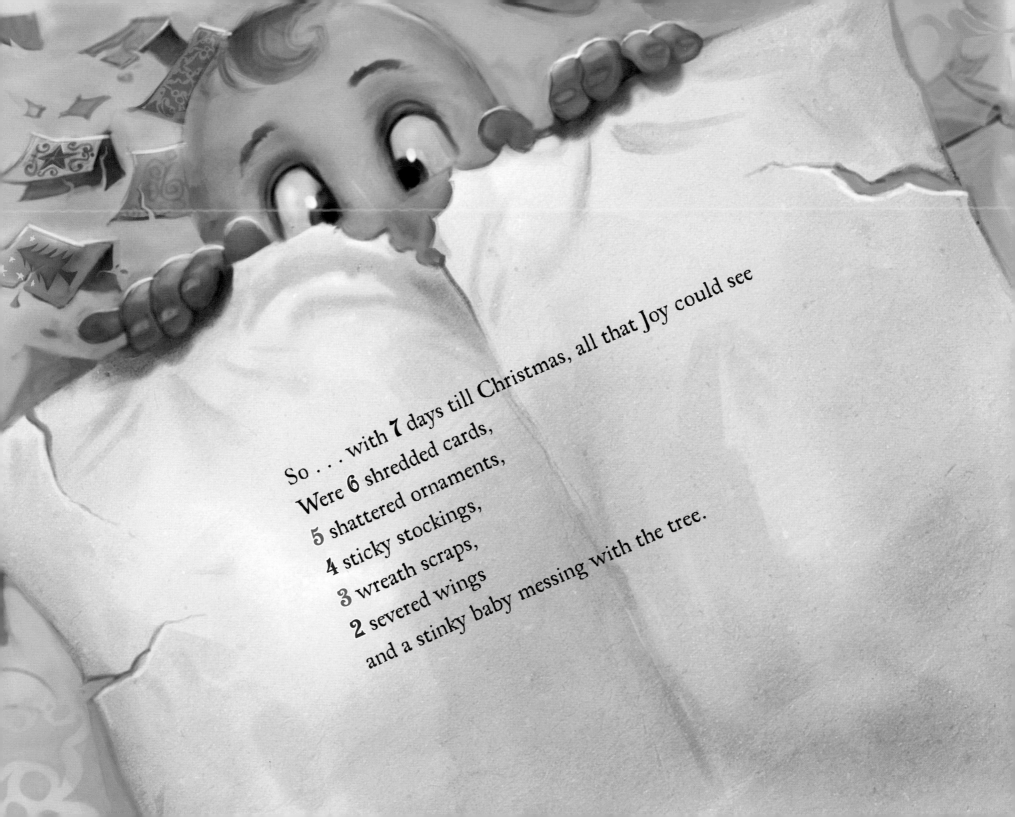

So . . . with **7** days till Christmas, all that Joy could see

Were **6** shredded cards,

5 shattered ornaments,

4 sticky stockings,

3 wreath scraps,

2 severed wings

and a stinky baby messing with the tree.

Outside, Joy built her snowmen, all lined up on the hill.
Dad took Sam sledding . . . and they took a spill.

So . . . with **6** days till Christmas, all that Joy could see

Were **7** flattened snowmen,

6 shredded cards,

5 shattered ornaments,

4 sticky stockings,

3 wreath scraps,

2 severed wings

and a stinky baby messing with the tree.

After Joy's Christmas reindeer were posed throughout the hall,
Sam wobbled up before a bumpy fall.

So . . . with **5** days till Christmas, all that Joy could see

Were 8 legless reindeer,

7 flattened snowmen,

6 shredded cards,

5 shattered ornaments,

4 sticky stockings,

3 wreath scraps,

2 severed wings

and a stinky baby messing with the tree.

Joy counted the candy canes to give her friends at school,
Then saw them in Sam's mouth, all wet with drool.

So . . . with 4 days till Christmas, all that Joy could see
Were 9 drooly candy canes,
8 legless reindeer,
7 flattened snowmen,
6 shredded cards,
5 shattered ornaments,
4 sticky stockings,
3 wreath scraps,
2 severed wings
and a stinky baby messing with the tree.

Joy drew the icing faces on all the gingerbread.
Sam snatched the batch and ate off all the heads.

So . . . with **3** days till Christmas, all that Joy could see
Were **10** headless monsters,
9 drooly candy canes,
8 legless reindeer,
7 flattened snowmen,
6 shredded cards,
5 shattered ornaments,
4 sticky stockings,
3 wreath scraps,
2 severed wings
and a stinky baby messing with the tree.

Joy came upon her presents all wrapped inside some bags.
Too bad that Sam could not read any tags.

So . . . with **2** days till Christmas, all that Joy could see
Were **11** wrecked surprises,
10 headless monsters,
9 drooly candy canes,
8 legless reindeer,
7 flattened snowmen,
6 shredded cards,
5 shattered ornaments,
4 sticky stockings,
3 wreath scraps,
2 severed wings
and a stinky baby messing with the tree.

At night, Joy tried to leave out a plate for Santa Claus.
But all the cookies landed in Sam's jaws.

So . . . with **1** day till Christmas, all that Joy could see
Were **12** soggy cookies,
11 wrecked surprises,
10 headless monsters,
9 drooly candy canes,
8 legless reindeer,
7 flattened snowmen,
6 shredded cards,
5 shattered ornaments,
4 sticky stockings,
3 wreath scraps,
2 severed wings
and a stinky baby messing with the tree.

oy finally exploded. "I've HAD it with Sam's firsts!
He's ruined this year's Christmas—**it's the WORST!**"

She stomped away to bed; she felt no Christmas cheer.
"Perhaps he won't be horrible next year."

hen Joy saw Sam at breakfast, she glowered at the boy . . .

But had a change of heart when Sam said, **"JOY!"**

Joy grinned up at her parents, then happily confessed:
"With Sam here, this year's Christmas was the . . . **BEST!**"

On that Christmas morning, all that Joy could see
Were **12** Sam-kissed cookies,
11 rewrapped presents,
10 mended gingerbread,
9 replacement candy canes,
8 patched-up reindeer,
7 rebuilt snowmen,
6 cards' confetti,
5 taped-up ornaments,
4 unstuck stockings,
3 wreath swags,
2 reglued wings
and a **LOVELY** baby . . .

. . . stinking
up the tree.